# MR. CLU

by Roger Hargreaves

With love to Nayom
from Grandma
Barbara
April 2 005.

WORLD INTERNATIONAL

It was a rather nice morning.

In the sky the sun was up.

Shining.

In the trees the birds were up.

Singing.

But, in a rather scruffy house in the middle of a field, somebody wasn't up.

Can you guess who that somebody might be?

His alarm clock went off.

Mr Clumsy woke up, and reached out an arm to switch off his alarm clock.

And knocked it on to the floor.

"Whoops," he said. "That's the third alarm clock I've broken this week."

Mr Clumsy, as you might have guessed, was a rather clumsy fellow.

He got out of bed and switched on the radio.

The knob came off in his hand.

"Whoops," he said. "That's the second radio I've broken this month."

He went downstairs.

The postman had been, and there was a letter waiting for Mr Clumsy, lying on his doormat.

He picked it up, and went into his kitchen.

"First things first," he said, and took a slice of bread out of his bread bin and popped it into his toaster.

"Now," he thought, "I wonder who this letter is from?"

He looked at the letter in his hand.

But the letter wasn't in his hand.

What was in his hand was a slice of bread!

"I don't understand it," he said. "Where's the letter gone?"

Can you guess where the letter had gone?

That's right!

He'd put the letter in the toaster instead of the bread!

And there it was, browning nicely.

"Whoops," he said fishing it out.

"Ouch," he said, dropping it. "It's hot!"

Mr Clumsy bent down to pick the letter up.

But, in doing so, he banged his forehead on his kitchen table, and in doing so, he fell forwards and got his head stuck in the bread bin!

All of which wasn't surprising really.

As we said, he was a rather clumsy fellow.

In fact, he was a very clumsy fellow.

Actually, he was the clumsiest person in the world!

That very same morning, after he'd managed to get the bread bin off his head, Mr Clumsy went to town.

Shopping.

"First things first," he said, and went into the bank to get some money.

And somehow, while he was in the bank, Mr Clumsy, while he was writing a cheque, managed to spill ink all over the bank manager.

"Whoops," said Mr Clumsy.

He went into the butcher's.

"Morning Butcher," he said, cheerily.

And then he somehow managed to trip over his shoelaces, and somehow managed to fall into the butcher's shop window, and somehow managed to finish up with a string of sausages round his neck!

"Whoops," he said.

Mr Clumsy's next call was the supermarket.

Just inside the door there was a huge pyramid pile of cans of soup.

Well.

You can imagine what happened, can't you?

"Mmm," exclaimed Mr Clumsy. "Soup would be nice for supper," and he picked up a can.

Not a can from the top of the pile.

Oh no, not Mr Clumsy.

"Whoops," said Mr Clumsy, and went on his way.

Rubbing his head.

On his way home, he called in at the farm for some eggs.

And somehow, while he was crossing the farmyard, he managed to trip up.

And somehow, as he was falling, he managed to grab hold of the farmer.

And somehow, they both managed to finish up in the duckpond!

SPLASH!

"Whoops," said Mr Clumsy.

"Please," said the farmer as they sat together in the duckpond. "In future can I deliver your eggs to you?"

"That's extraordinarily kind of you," replied Mr Clumsy.

"Don't mention it," muttered the farmer.

Mr Clumsy went home.

"First things first," he said, and went for a bath.

But, as he was stepping into his bath, his foot somehow managed to slip on the soap, and he somehow managed to turn a somersault, and he somehow managed to land with his head in the linen basket.

"Whoops!" said a muffled voice.

Later, he went downstairs for supper.

Soup, from the supermarket.

Sausages, from the butcher's.

And eggs, from the farm.

Or rather.

Soup, from the saucepan that had boiled over.

Sausages, from the frying pan that had caught fire.

And eggs, oh dear, very very very scrambled eggs!

A normal Mr Clumsy sort of supper.

"That was nice," he said, leaning back in his chair.

CRASH!

"Whoops!" said Mr Clumsy, "I think I'd better go
to bed."

And he did.

And that is the end of the story.

"Goodnight, Mr Clumsy!"

Mr Clumsy leaned over to turn off his bedside light, and . . .

Oh dear.

"Whoops!"

# 3 Great Offers For Mr Men Fans

## 1 FREE Door Hangers and Posters

In every Mr Men and Little Miss Book like this one you will find a special token. Collect 6 and we will send you either a brilliant Mr. Men or Little Miss poster and a Mr Men or Little Miss double sided, full colour, bedroom door hanger. Apply using the coupon overleaf, enclosing six tokens and a 50p coin for your choice of two items.

Egmont World tokens can be used towards any other Egmont World / World International token scheme promotions, in early learning and story / activity books.

**Posters:** Tick your preferred choice of either Mr Men ☐ or Little Miss ☐

**Door Hangers: Choose from:** Mr. Nosey & Mr Muddle ☐, Mr Greedy & Mr Lazy ☐, Mr Tickle & Mr Grumpy ☐, Mr Slow & Mr Busy ☐, Mr Messy & Mr Quiet ☐, Mr Perfect & Mr Forgetful ☐, Little Miss Fun & Little Miss Late ☐, Little Miss Helpful & Little Miss Tidy ☐, Little Miss Busy & Little Miss Brainy ☐, Little Miss Star & Little Miss Fun ☐.
**(Please tick)**

ENTRANCE FEE 3 SAUSAGES
MR. GREEDY

## 2 Mr Men Library Boxes

Keep your growing collection of Mr Men and Little Miss books in these superb library boxes. With an integral carrying handle and stay-closed fastener, these full colour, plastic boxes are fantastic. They are just £5.49 each including postage. Order overleaf.

## 3 Join The Club

To join the fantastic Mr Men & Little Miss Club, check out the page overleaf NOW!

• RETURN THIS WHOLE PAGE •

# Join Our Club!

**MR. MEN & Little Miss CLUB**

When you become a member of the fantastic Mr Men and Little Miss Club you'll receive a personal letter from Mr Happy and Little Miss Giggles, a club badge with your name, and a superb Welcome Pack (pictured below right).

You'll also get birthday and Christmas cards from the Mr Men and Little Misses, 2 newsletters crammed with special offers, privileges and news, and a copy of the 12 page Mr Men catalogue which includes great party ideas.

If it were on sale in the shops, the Welcome Pack alone might cost around £13. But a year's membership is just £9.99 (plus 73p postage) with a 14 day money-back guarantee if you are not delighted!

**HOW TO APPLY** To apply for any of these three great offers, ask an adult to complete the coupon below and send it with appropriate payment and tokens (where required) to: Mr Men Offers, PO Box 7, Manchester M19 2HD. Credit card orders for Club membership ONLY by telephone, please call: 01403 242727.

To be completed by an adult

❑ **1.** Please send a poster and door hanger as selected overleaf. I enclose six tokens and a 50p coin for post (coin not required if you are also taking up 2. or 3. below).

❑ **2.** Please send __ Mr Men Library case(s) and __ Little Miss Library case(s) at £5.49 each.

❑ **3.** Please enrol the following in the Mr Men & Little Miss Club at £10.72 (inc postage)

Fan's Name:_____Fan's Address:_____

_____Post Code:_____Date of birth: __/__/__

Your Name:_____Your Address:_____

Post Code:_____Name of parent or guardian (if not you):_____

Total amount due: £_____ (£5.49 per Library Case, £10.72 per Club membership)

❑ I enclose a cheque or postal order payable to Egmont World Limited.

❑ Please charge my MasterCard / Visa account.

Card number: | | | | | | | | | | | | | | | | |

Expiry Date: ____/____    Signature: _____

Data Protection Act: If you do **not** wish to receive other family offers from us or companies we recommend, please tick this box ❑. Offer applies to UK only